Encyclopedia of Strange Looking Animals
Published by Moppet Books
Los Angeles, California

ISBN: 978-1-7337921-4-1

Art direction and book design by Melissa Medina
Written by Fredrik Colting and Melissa Medina

Printed in China

MOPPET BOOKS

MOPPETBOOKSPUBLISHING.COM

Encyclopedia *of* Strange Looking Animals

Volume Two

Written by

Fredrik Colting & Melissa Medina

Illustrated by Vlad Stankovic

Terra Creaturae

Land Creatures

Venezuelan Poodle Moth

The Venezuelan Poodle Moth was first photographed in 2009 by Kyrgyzstani zoologist Dr. Arthur Anker in Venezuela. It got its name for the obvious reason that it looks like a cross between a moth and a poodle. No other expeditions to the region have been able to spot the Poodle Moth again and some people think it doesn't really exist. However, thousands of new insects are discovered every year in the South American rainforests, so it's very possible that it is entirely real, although incredibly rare. For the sake of all the fanclubs that have sprung up online for this adorable little fluffer, let's hope so.

Number 1

Panda Ant

Speaking of cute but strange insects, let's talk about Panda Ants. Panda Ants are actually not ants at all, but a type of wasp found in dry coastal regions of Chile. Like many wasp species, and unlike true ants, Panda Ants do not live in colonies or have queens or workers. Panda Ants get their name from the dramatic black and white coloration of the females, and because the females don't have wings, they look more like ants. But don't be fooled by the cute, fuzzy, bear-like appearance—they are also known as "Cow Killer Ants" because of the incredibly painful sting the females can deliver from a long stinger.

Number 2

Glass Frog

Glass Frogs live in trees along rivers in Central and South America. These little frogs are lime green and look pretty normal from above. But if you look at them from below, you'll see that they have an amazing feature: The skin on their bellies and legs is invisible! That is, it's transparent, which means you can see their heart, liver, veins, and lots of other weird stuff through their skin.

Number 3

Indian Purple Frog

The Indian Purple Frog is a funny-looking frog that lives most of its life underground near streams in the Western Ghats of India. It actually only emerges for a few weeks each year during the monsoon, for mating. These frogs are a dark purplish-grey in color with blob-shaped bodies, small heads and oddly pointed snouts. The sound it makes is also strange, as it sounds like a chicken clucking! In some tribal communities, a good luck charm is made from the frog and worn by children, as it is believed this will reduce their fear of storms. We think everyone should just leave this strange blobby frog alone for the few days it comes out to play in the rain.

Number 4

Mata Mata

The Mata Mata is a large freshwater turtle found in South America, primarily in the Amazon River. It's an odd looking turtle as it has a rough and knobby shell, a large, flat, triangular-shaped head, a long neck with a bunch of warty protrusions, and a pointy horn-shaped snout. It mostly just lies around doing nothing but waiting for food to drift by. This works well because its body looks like a piece of bark and its head like leaves, giving it an effective camouflage. When something yummy swims by, it simply opens its large mouth as wide as possible, creating a vacuum that sucks in the prey. So even though being lazy isn't something we usually associate with success, it seems to work for the Mata Mata turtle!

Number 5

Superb Bird-of-Paradise

Also called the Greater Lophorina, the Superb Bird-of-Paradise lives in the rainforests of Indonesia and New Guinea. For some reason there are more males than females, so the males, over time, have developed a certain behavior to stand out: They dance. First, they prepare a "dance floor" by sweeping the dirt with leaves. The male then spreads his folded black feather cape and blue-green breast shield, while snapping his tail feathers together. The average male has to dance like this for as many as 20 females before they find one that is impressed enough to say yes. It's hard work being a Superb Bird-of-Paradise!

Number 6

Long-Wattled Umbrellabird

The Long-Wattled Umbrellabird is quite the looker, and he knows it. Both males and females have an impressive umbrella-like crest on top of their heads. But the adult males really stand out with their thick-feathered, inflatable wattle dangling from their throat. It can be extended to an astonishing length, or retracted in flight. These crazy looking wattles actually help to amplify their low, booming mating calls. Sightings are pretty rare, but if you're lucky, you can find them wattling along in the rainforests of western Ecuador and Colombia.

Number 7

Shoebill

The Shoebill is a large and rather terrifying East African bird with an oversized shoe-shaped beak. It's actually the third longest beak in the world and it enables them to hunt prey as big as baby crocodiles. Yes, this bird eats crocodiles! Another more gruesome fact is the way the shoebill uses the razor-sharp edges of its beak to behead their prey before eating them. Oh, and they also have a really creepy signature death stare. Knowing that, it's best not to try and shoo this bird away!

Number 8

King Vulture

The King Vulture lives in forests stretching from southern Mexico to northern Argentina, where it can soar in the air for hours, barely flapping its large wings. It's a colorful bird with yellow, orange, blue, purple, and red skin, as well as a very noticeable orange fleshy bit on its beak. It's often depicted in Mayan art and it was named after a legendary Mayan vulture king who served as a messenger between humans and the gods. The King Vulture is a scavenger and has a strong and sharp beak that can cut through the hide of a carcass. Don't mess with the King!

Number 9

Spiny Bush Viper

The Spiny Bush Viper is a venomous snake native to Africa, specifically Congo, Uganda, and Kenya. They are usually green with a yellow belly and their bodies are covered with large, flaky-looking scales. They live in rainforests where they ambush their prey by hanging upside down from a branch and jumping on it to inject their venom. The venom causes severe bleeding of inner organs, so they don't make good pets for obvious reasons. But, luckily for us humans, they mostly eat rodents, birds, lizards, and frogs. Mostly.

Number 10

Naked Mole-Rat

The Naked Mole-Rat is a small burrowing rodent with somewhat translucent, wrinkly pink or grayish-pink skin. This little rodent, native to parts of East Africa, has a LOT of strange and cool features. For instance, it is the only known cold-blooded mammal, it has no external ears, almost no eyesight, and no pain sensitivity in its skin. It is resistant to cancer and oxygen deprivation. It also never drinks water, can live up to 30 years, and can move each of its front teeth separately, like a pair of chopsticks. In other words, it's a great friend to bring to a sushi place!

Number 11

Lowland Streaked Tenrec

The Lowland Streaked Tenrec is found in Madagascar and it looks sort of like a small hedgehog with a long snout and a spine-covered coat. Its favorite food is earthworms, which it tricks into coming up to the surface by stomping on the ground. On its back it has something called quills, which it can rub together to produce a high-pitched ultrasonic sound—and it's the only known mammal to do so! So, to summarize: It's a music-making, spike-shielded, dancing, hedgehog-type animal that eats earthworms. Pretty cool if you ask us.

Number 12

Markhor

The Markhor is the largest species in the goat family and it lives in northern Pakistan. It's actually their national animal. Their corkscrew-shaped horns can measure up to 63 inches (160 centimeters) and are used to dig for food and to fight with other males. They live on mountainsides and are expert climbers. A less flattering quality is that Markhors smell really bad. So, if you are ever lucky to be near one, you'll probably smell it before you see it!

Number 13

Saiga Antelope

The Saiga Antelope is a very strange-looking antelope that roams the dry steppes or semi-desert grasslands of Russia and Kazakhstan, although not many can be found as they are critically endangered. What really sets these antelopes apart is their long, accordian-looking nose! This schnozzle isn't just for looks though. It helps filter out dust kicked up by the herd and cools their blood during hot summer months. Saiga Antelope are also very fast and can run up to 48 miles per hour (80 km/h). You try that with an inflatable nose!

Number 14

Philippine Tarsier

The Philippine Tarsier is named after where it lives (duh, the Philippines) and after its elongated tarsus, which is an ankle bone. This allows the Tarsier to jump 10 feet (3 meters) from tree to tree. There's actually a lot that's unusual about the Tarsier, but one especially odd thing is their eyes. Tarsiers have the largest eye-to-body size ratio of all mammals, but they can't move them around. Instead they rotate their entire head 180°. If humans had equally large eyes, they would be as big as grapefruits!

Number 15

Mandrill

The Mandrill lives in tropical rainforests in southern Gabon, Cameroon, Equatorial Guinea, and Congo, and is the heaviest living monkey, weighing up to 119 pounds (54 kg). They live in very large groups called "hordes," some as big as 1000 Mandrills! What makes Mandrills so strange (and beautiful) looking are their wildly bright colors. They have long, bright red noses with blue ridges that fan out on the sides, a yellow beard, and a rainbow colored rump! No other mammal in the world is known to have red and blue pigments like that, which makes these special monkies truly a work of art.

Number 16

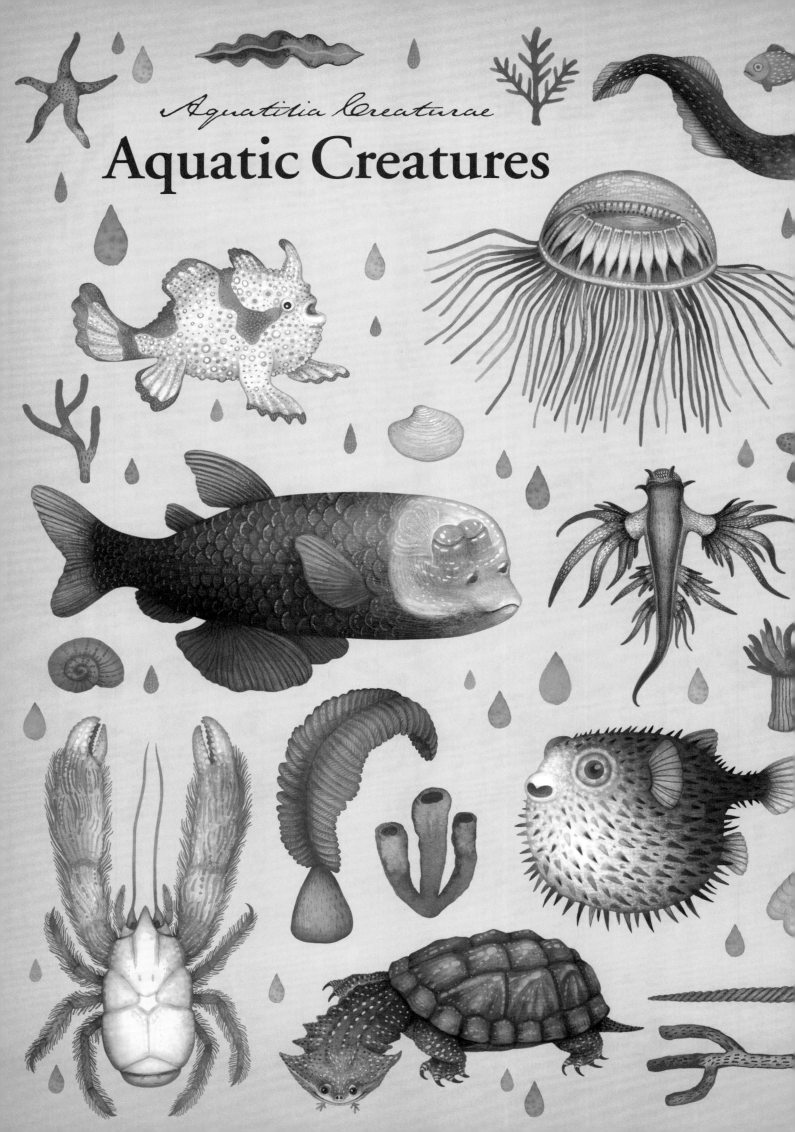

Aquatilia Creaturae
Aquatic Creatures

Yeti Crab

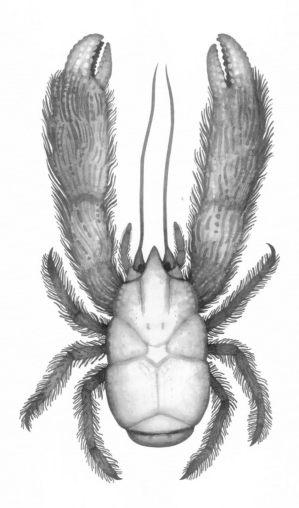

The Kiwa Hirsute, or Yeti Crab, is white with silky blond fur and can be found in the South Pacific. It lives in clusters over hot water springs deep on the bottom of the ocean. They are virtually blind, so they couldn't see each other even if they were colored like the rainbow! But they do have something most animals don't—a built-in food factory. The Yeti Crab's hairy "arms" capture all kinds of bacteria that live and grow there, which is actually its primary source of food. We wish cookies would grow on our arms!

Number 17

Glaucus Atlanticus

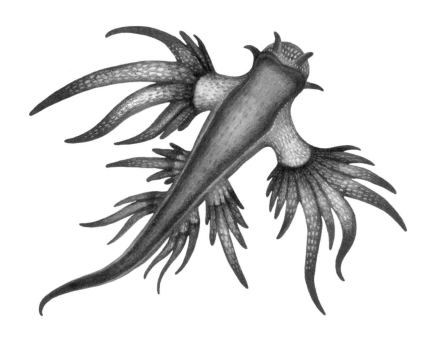

The Glaucus Atlanticus, also called the Blue Sea Dragon, is a species of small brightly-colored sea slug that can be found throughout the Atlantic, Pacific, and Indian Oceans. These little guys are only around 1.2 inches (3 cm), but are smarter than your average slug. They float upside down, carried along by the ocean currents, with the blue side of their body facing upwards and blending in with the blue of the water, and the silver side facing downwards and blending in with the sunlight reflecting on the ocean's surface from below. This is a great camouflaging tool. They also eat poisonous animals, like the Portuguese Man o' War, and collect their stinging cells to use as a defense against predators. Go Team GA!

Number 18

Axolotl

The Axolotl, also known as the Mexican walking fish, is actually not a fish at all but a salamander, which is an amphibian. This species' only natural habitat is the lakes and canals under Mexico City. Sadly, there are now just a few hundred left in the wild, although tens of thousands can be found in home aquariums and research laboratories around the world. Axolotls are wildly popular due to their cute faces that appear to be smiling, their feathery headdresses (which are actually gills), and their amazing ability to regrow limbs, and even organs, in just a few weeks! Excuse me, Mr. Axolotl...you dropped your arm there.

Number 19

Mantis Shrimp

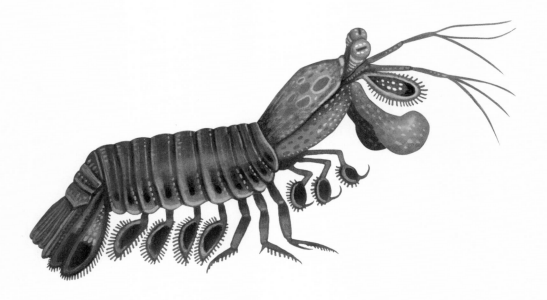

The Mantis Shrimp are one of the most fearsome creatures in the ocean...except they are not actually shrimp but stomatopods, distant relatives to crabs, shrimp, and lobsters. They use two dactyl clubs, which are like bony fists, to smash through crab shells and other prey. These clubs shoot out at 50 miles per hour (80 km/h), accelerating faster than a bullet, which actually makes the surrounding water briefly reach the temperature of the Sun's surface! This is why, when aquariums have them in their collection, they must be kept behind shatterproof acrylic glass or they could break it. So yeah, don't call them a shrimp unless you're lookin' for a fight!

Number 20

Number 20

Sea Pen

As their name suggests, Sea Pens often look like those old-timey feathery writing pens. These delicate, colorful, underwater animals are actually a type of soft coral, and a single sea pen is both an individual and a colony. Some can do cool things like emit a bright greenish light when touched and rapidly deflate to hide from predators. Sea Pens are found worldwide, in super shallow to super deep waters. So basically anywhere you go, you could find a Pen lying around.

Number 21

Dumbo Octopus

The Dumbo Octopus is a type of sea umbrella octopus that lives in depths of at least 13,000 feet (4,000 m), making it the deepest living of all known octopuses. They come in various shapes, sizes, and colors and can even change color to camouflage themselves with the ocean floor. They are known for their fins, which resemble Disney's Dumbo the elephant's ears. That's actually how they move around, by slowly flapping their ear-like fins (just like Dumbo!). But unlike Dumbo the elephant, these little guys are on average just 8 to 12 inches long. So cuuute!

Number 22

Halitrephes Jelly

The Halitrephes Jelly, also known as the firework jellyfish, lives at a depth of 5,000 feet (1500 m) in both temperate and tropical waters, in Baja, Mexico, the Atlantic, the Mediterranean, and even the Antarctic. Not a whole lot is known about this species, but when researchers first discovered it, they saw what looked like a real-life underwater firework exploding right in front of them. When illuminated by a light, the Halitrephes Jelly turns brilliant colors of pink and yellow to make it look like the large burst of a massive Fourth of July firework. Interestingly, without any lights, it's almost invisible because of its translucency. Happy 4th of Jelly!

Number 23

Macropinna Microstoma

Macropinna Microstoma, or the Barreleye fish, is one of the strangest looking fish in the world. It has a transparent, fluid-filled dome on its head and tubular eyes that are really good at detecting light. This is helpful because they live in the northern Pacific Ocean at depths of over 2,000 feet (600 meters), where it's pitch black.

Number 24

This small, strange fish (only 4 to 6 inches in length) can rotate its green tubular eyes straight up to look for shadows of small fish and jellyfish to eat—just like looking through a glass roof. Hey, Mr. Barreleye, we can see what you're thinking!

Number 24

Sea Lamprey

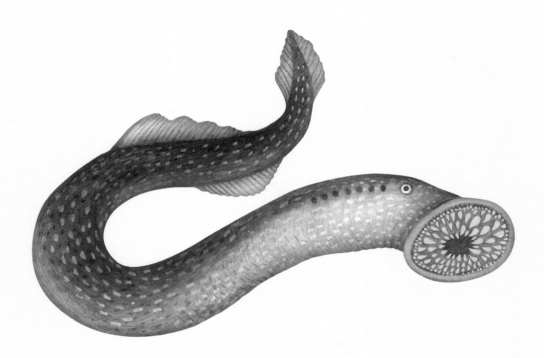

The Sea Lamprey is a parasitic jawless fish also referred to as the "vampire fish," which is easy to understand when you see its mouth. It sits at the end of an eel-like body and has a round opening with sharp teeth arranged in circular rows. They use these suction cup-like mouths to attach themselves to the skin of a fish and then they begin to rasp away tissue with their sharp, probing tongue, eating away at the fish's insides. It sounds like a mix between an alien and a zombie—good thing Sea Lamprey's don't live on land! Where they do live is in the northern and western Atlantic Ocean, and some parts of Europe, where they are actually considered a delicacy. They are even served pickled in Finland.

Number 25

Blue Parrotfish

The Blue Parrotfish lives on coral reefs in shallow water in the tropical and subtropical parts of the western Atlantic Ocean and the Caribbean Sea. They have a big beak, just like a parrot, that is actually part of a set of teeth that are so strong they can grind ingested rocks into sand. In just one year, one Parrotfish can chew up a ton of coral into sand. Just don't teach them how to speak or you'll hear "Polly want a cracker!" every time you go swimming.

Number 26

Japanese Spider Crab

The Japanese Spider Crab is the largest crustacean on Earth, spanning up to 12.1 feet (3.7 meters) from the tip of one front claw to the other. They're also one of the world's largest arthropods, which are animals with external skeletons, and one of the longest living creatures in the world, living up to 100 years! As the Spider Crab keeps growing, it needs to shed its exoskeleton (that's called molting), and it basically crawls out of it to grow a new one, leaving the old, empty shell behind. They live in the waters around Japan and use camouflage to keep their big bodies out of sight by attaching sponges and other animals to their shells. They are reported to have a gentle disposition despite their ferocious appearance.

Number 27

Pufferfish

The Pufferfish family includes many species that all have the ability to puff up when being threatened. They do this by filling their very elastic stomachs with water. Once inflated, spikes on their bodies stand straight out, causing most predators to think twice before they take a bite out of it. But if they do, they'll quickly learn that most pufferfish are equipped with a toxic substance called tetrodotoxin. In fact, in Japan, where eating pufferfish is considered a delicacy, many people die every year from accidentally eating a poisoned piece of fish. Tetrodotoxin deadens the tongue and lips, and induces dizziness and vomiting, eventually leading to muscle paralysis. Not something you want from your fish sticks!

Number 28

Warty Frogfish

The Warty Frogfish clearly did not have any luck being named, or with the fact that its skin is covered with small, wart-like bumps. What they do have going for them is the capacity to change color and pattern to blend in with their environment, mouths that open wide enough to allow them to consume prey the same size as themselves, and a built-in fishing rod in their dorsal spine that dangles a lure in front of their mouths that looks like a small fish. When another fish swims up to take the lure, WHAM! they swallow it whole. They also have cool pectoral and pelvic fins that act almost like feet that move them along the bottom of coral reefs. It's almost worth the warts!

Number 29

Narwhal

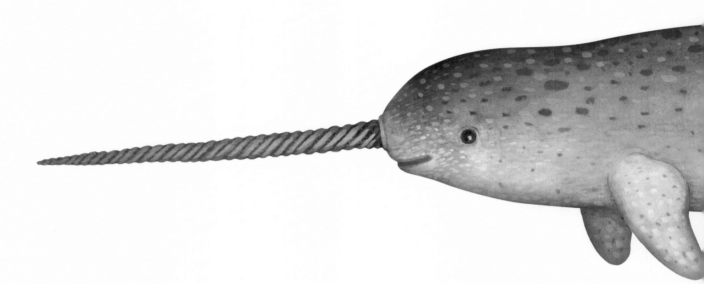

The Narwhal is a medium-sized whale that lives year-round in the Arctic waters around Greenland, Canada, and Russia. It has a large, spiralled "tusk," that is actually a tooth that can grow as long as 10 feet (3 m). That's the reason they are dubbed "unicorns of the sea." The tusks are a sensory organ with millions of nerve endings, and this is how narwhals communicate, by rubbing their tusks against one another.

Number 30

They also speak regular "whale" using clicks, whistles, and knocks under water. Speaking of under water, narwhals can dive very deep, up to 4,920 feet (1,500 m) and stay down there for up to 25 minutes. Very impressive, but we can't stop thinking about what it would be like to have a tooth 10 feet long!

Number 30

End of Volume Two

We sure hope you've enjoyed learning about these strange looking animals.

Stay tuned for Volume Three!